Valletta and the Year of Changes

Simone Mansell Broome

PRETTY PUG PUBLISHING

EST. 2020

ISBN 978-1-8384494-1-4
First published in 2021 by Pretty Pug Publishing

Pretty Pug Publishing
26 The Seed Warehouse
Poole Quay BH15 1SB

IN DEDICATION

This book is dedicated to Roger for his continued and unflagging positivity, support and feedback, and to four little Welsh-born 'mice', Orla, Erica, Martha and Cassian.

Simone Mansell Broome

In memory of Susan - my wonderfully humorous, artistic Mum.

Cerys Susannah Rees

Chapter 1
The Changes Begin

Valletta and Oslo were not ordinary mice. They were sister and brother mice who lived with their parents in a mouse-sized house under the floorboards. These floorboards were in the living-room of 46 Spring Blossom Road. Like I said, Valletta and Oslo were not ordinary mice.

'You,' said Great Uncle Leningrad to both of them, 'belong to a very special mouse family. You are part of the Stowaway Clan. Our history goes back for hundreds of years. For we are brave and adventurous mice, and we like to see the world.'

This was true. Aunt Florence, one of Great Uncle Leningrad and Great Auntie Sofia's four children, was an artist. Her job was to look after a very precious old map of the world, which was stretched out under the floorboards of the human children's bedroom in Spring Blossom Road. Someone in the mouse family, a long time ago, had copied this map from one that the humans had. Aunt Florence marked in the bits which faded, with ink she made from marmite or jam. She also painted a perfect pawprint by every place that a Stowaway mouse had visited.

Aunt Florence used paintbrushes made especially for her by Bergen, her cousin. Bergen, who was often called Berg or Bergie by his family, was Valletta and Oslo's dad. Bergen made each paintbrush out of a cocktail stick sliver with a single whisker cut into two pieces. Half the whisker became the bristle of the paintbrush and the other half tied it tightly to the stick.

There were lots of painted pawprints on the map. Wherever the humans went – and they did go out and about and around and away a lot – a Stowaway mouse went too, in secret. The mice stowed away on trips to the park, to the beach, to visit other mice, or for Summer Holidays! These Summer Holidays were Valletta and Oslo's favourite times of the year, apart from Christmouse. The young mice started getting excited about Summer Holidays as soon as the decorations came down and the very last crumbs of mince pie were gone.

Great Auntie Sofia had a beautiful singing voice, and she sang or spoke a Stowaway rhyme while she knitted. The children loved hearing it and sometimes joined in.

'We're the Stowaways, the Stowaways;
we like to travel, to go away.
We creep into their bags and cases
and then we visit lovely places.
We can go by car, or go by bus;
all kinds of boats are fine with us,
and if our humans ride by train,
we little mice do not complain.
Just beware if they talk of flights!
Those metal birds give mice a fright!'

One March day, an unusual thing happened. Great Uncle Leningrad called a meeting at the house under the floorboards which he shared with his wife, Sofia, and his daughter, Florence. All of the other Stowaway mice who lived at 46 Spring Blossom Road were invited to come; Jersey, Annécy and their children, Malaga and Sark, Aaron, Guernsey and Aaron's daughter Nancy, as well as Bergen and Vienna and their children, Oslo and Valletta. This meeting was at ten o'clock one Fursday morning.

Oslo said, 'If Great Uncle Leningrad wants to see us all together, in the same place, it must be a MICIS.' That's a crisis in mousespeak, or something **very important** anyway.

'Whatever!' said Valletta, who sometimes found her brother a bit boring.

Everyone did come. Great Uncle Leningrad seemed to be in charge, as he generally was. He was wearing his glasses and looking serious. Great Auntie Sofia sat in a corner humming gently. She'd brought her knitting with her, in case her husband **went on too long**, which he sometimes did.

As well as being good at painting and drawing, Aunt Florence also had extremely neat handwriting.

Great Uncle Leningrad had told her to bring a pad and pencil with her to the meeting. She did as she was asked to, then sat next to him.

'Florence will take notes so we will all know what's what,' said Leningrad. Florence blushed under her fur.

'Shall we begin, my fellow mice? The humans are doing strange things. They have stopped going out to work and to school. Their car stays in the garage all the time. They are here **all day** and **every day**.'

'No, they're not,' said Valletta. 'They still go shopping.' Valletta liked food rather a lot. Vienna, her mother, once told Great Auntie Sofia that Valletta 'ate like a horse' and that it was a **good thing** she used up so much energy. Valletta thought these were silly things to say.

'The cupboard under the stairs is full of toilet rolls and cans of groceries like baked beans and tomatoes,' went on Great Uncle Leningrad. 'They are panic-buying, which means they are buying much more than usual.'

'But why does that matter dear?' asked Great Auntie

Sofia, dropping several stitches.

'Panic-buying, my dearest one, is what humans do when they think something bad is happening or going to happen. It's what they do before a war starts. Or a bank holiday.' Everyone thought about this for a minute or two.

'And the cupboards are full of crinkly packets of pasta too', said Nancy, who was one of Valletta and Oslo's cousins. 'Some of them are shaped like bows.'

The adult mice all smiled at Nancy, who also had a healthy appetite and who was fond of bows, frills and sparkly clothes. Unlike Valletta. When she thought no-one was looking, Valletta poked her tiny mouse tongue out at her cousin.

'The humans have become very noisy,' said Valletta.

'I can't hear myself think,' said Vienna, and all the other adult mice smiled again.

'This,' said Great Uncle Leningrad, 'is something called 'lockdown' and we mice must be careful. We must adapt, work together and be very clever.'

Everyone looked at him. There was no more poking out of tongues, knitting, humming or chatting in corners.

'We must forage at night, not in the daytime,' he went on, 'unless we are sure, quite sure, that the humans have **all** gone out shopping or for their daily walk. And we must be quiet and rest or sleep when they are around, otherwise…'

'We'll go hungry,' said Nancy and Valletta together. It was unusual for the two of them to speak at the same time, or even to agree about something.

'Yes,' said Great Uncle Leningrad, 'the children are correct. We will go hungry, but even worse, we may be discovered. And that would be the end of our travels and it would be the end of us.'

Everyone listened to Leningrad and took notice of what he said. Every single mouse changed his or her routine. Helped by Bergen, Great Uncle Leningrad organised rotas for night time food hunting. They drew up charts and timetables, lists of quiet things to keep the little mice busy and cheerful things to stop them from becoming too bored or too grumpy.

All mouse outings and adventures stopped. The mice stayed at home. Singing and rumbunctious rodent-y games became very, very rare treats for when the coast was clear of humans.

At first, it was dreadful and all the small mice complained and moaned. But they did get used to it. They didn't like the way their mousey lives had changed, but it became sort of normal. Then, three things happened which made the mouse family's lives a little better.

The first thing was that Great Auntie Sofia knitted earmuffs, mouse-sized earmuffs, for her family to wear when all of the human rumpus above the floorboards just got **too much**. Because, of course, life had changed above the floorboards for the humans as well!

The second good thing was **baking**. Suddenly, the humans were baking bread, pies, biscuits, buns and cakes all of the time. The whole human family was doing this.

'And where there is baking,' said Great Auntie Sofia, 'no mouse will starve. There will be crumbs and more crumbs.' There were indeed crumbs and crusts and leftover bits every day. Nomouse could complain that he or she was hungry at all.

And the third good thing was the Fursday clapping. Each Fursday evening the human family went into their back garden, taking with them pots, pans, spoons and ladles and all sorts of metal things from their kitchen. Then they made lots of noise, for about ten minutes. When they stopped banging metal things, they clapped their hands loudly. Because there was such a big human racket going on, the mouse family were able to creep out and clap and bang and cheer and join in with the general noise-making in their own mousey way. The humans didn't notice them.

'But why are we clapping?' asked Valletta, who like to know the reason for doing things. She had what the grown-ups called 'an enquiring mind'.

'I'm not sure,' said Great Uncle Leningrad, 'but I think they are saying well done, and thank you, and please-carry-on-doing-whatever-it-is-you're-doing to some brave people who are working hard to make this lockdown thing go away. So we Stowaway mice must do our bit too, once a week, just like the humans.'

Mouse life was very different now. Sometimes the children were fed up and sad, and then they were mean to each other. Sometimes the adult mice felt frightened about the future. How long would all this strangeness last? For how long could they keep their little mice quiet, and safe? However much the adult mice twirled their whiskers, or stretched and rearranged their tails, they still couldn't answer these questions.

Chapter 2
Good Days and a Bad Day for Valletta

All the Stowaway mice missed going out and going away. They missed putting new pawprints on the map under the floorboards, when they returned home from faraway places. Oslo and Valletta talked to each other about holidays.

'Are we going to have a holiday this year?' asked Oslo.

'It's not fair if we don't have one,' said Valletta. 'I don't want all this justthesameness. I want something good to look forward to.'

April, May, June and July came and went, but finally, in August, they did have a little holiday. For a week. One evening, the whole family of mice crept into a great heap of bags and cases which were piled up in the hall of the humans' house at 46 Spring Blossom Road.

Not quite the whole family. Leningrad and Sofia decided to stay behind to 'hold the fort,' whatever that means. The next morning both humans and mice travelled together in the big red Volvo to a cottage on a farm in the countryside.

'It's not quite what we're used to,' said Vienna to Bergen, when they had arrived and had crept quietly out of all the bags, cases, picnic hampers and wellington boots which had been unpacked into the hall of the holiday cottage.

Bergen spotted a hole in the floorboards, where he told the other adults to take the little ones and hide, until he and Valletta had worked out the best place for them all to stay for the week. They decided on the larder, a large cupboard next to the kitchen. It had nooks and crannies and hidey holes. What's more there was a little window which was kept slightly open. They could use that to climb out into the garden and the fields beyond it. The other special thing about the larder was that there was just so much food for the mice! Despite the huge supply of food, it looked to Bergen and Vienna that their children Oslo and Valletta, the oldest two of the five little mice, were wearing their 'whatever' looks, and that even the younger mice weren't quite as excited as they usually were at the beginning of a holiday.

'I think we might have all become a little spoilt with the way things used to be,' said Bergen. 'Especially Oslo and Valletta, who are old enough to remember life before we all had to stay at home. We will have fresh air, and long walks, and the change will do all of us good.'

He was right. They all had a wonderful time in their cottage on the farm. It turned out to be just as much fun as their other holidays, even though it wasn't nearly such a long distance away from home.

The children missed Great Uncle Leningrad and Great Auntie Sofia. When the mice returned with the humans in the Volvo, Valletta, Oslo and their three cousins rushed round to see their great-uncle and great-aunt.

'How was your holiday?' asked Sofia. 'Did you have a good time?'

'It was amazing,' said Nancy. 'We made dens, dams

and went fishing.'

'And got muddy and had battles and barbecues and a bonfire. It was so much better than I thought it would be,' said Valletta.

Suddenly, Oslo stopped grinning and looked a little bit worried. 'Does this mean we're back to normal again now, Uncle?'

'I'm afraid not,' said the older mouse, shaking his head. 'You've been lucky. You've had a chance to get away for a holiday, and we all know how important travel is to us Stowaways. But who knows what the colder weather will bring? We'll have to be strong and we'll have to wait and see.'

The children went quiet. They didn't like not knowing about the future. It made them anxious all over again.

'Should we still clap on Fursdays?' asked Valletta.

'Yes,' said Great Auntie Sofia. 'We'll keep clapping and you must try hard not to worry. We'll be warm and we'll have full bellies.'

'And each other,' said Oslo, holding both Great Uncle Leningrad and Great Auntie Sofia's paws in his.

'That's right dears,' said Great Auntie Sofia, smiling at Oslo and his younger sister Valletta. 'That will do perfectly for now. We mice can see the world again soon.'

Then Valletta started to say the encouraging Stowaway rhyme, and all the other mice joined in with her:

'We're the Stowaways, the Stowaways;
we like to travel, to go away.
We creep into their bags and cases
and then we visit lovely places.
We can go by car, or go by bus;
all kinds of boats are fine with us,
and if our humans ride by train,
we little mice do not complain.
Just beware if they talk of flights!
Those metal birds give mice a fright!'

One sunny September morning, Valletta Stowaway was not happy. Her day started badly and then it got worse. When she woke up, it felt like her whiskers had bent backwards during the night and were now pointing all over the place. Her mouth and cheeks felt tight and itchy.

Valletta's head was hurting too. In an I-haven't-had-a-good-sleep-and-now-I'm-cross sort of way.

'Oh dear,' said Bergen when his daughter grumped into the kitchen. 'Did you get out of bed the wrong side this morning?'

Valletta didn't bother answering. Her little bed was pushed right up against the wall. She could only get out on one side. Her dad wandered off. He had a tiny plank of wood in one paw and a busy look about him. Valletta walked up to her mother, who was wiping the plates from supper the night before, and putting them back up on the shelf.

'Such a lovely morning,' she said. 'It must be so bright outside. I feel like spring cleaning.'

'Oh, forgoodnesssake!' Valletta thought. 'She's laughing about having more work to do. And you don't spring clean when it's not spring. That's silly.'

It was in fact a very long time since the spring.

It also felt like a long time since August when

the mice, the whole family, (except for Great Uncle Leningrad and Great Auntie Sofia), had managed to go on a little holiday to the countryside. As they always did, they had stowed away in the bags and rucksacks, picnic hampers and cases, and even inside welly boots, which the humans piled in the back of their red Volvo car.

Valletta had hoped to herself that when they came back from the holiday, their world at 46 Spring Blossom Road would have quietly slipped back to the way it was before March. March was when this strange human thing called 'lockdown' began. But nothing had changed back to how it used to be. Valletta was fed up. This morning she was cross too.

Her brother Oslo was sitting at the kitchen table drawing pictures of cars. He was also working on a very complicated picture of the tractor on the farm where they'd stayed on holiday.

'We're having an Indian Summer now,' said Valletta's mother Vienna, to nobody except herself. 'But you can feel the frost is just around the corner.'

Valletta rolled her eyes and made a sort of

harrumphing sound. 'Make up your mind, won't you,' she whispered to herself. 'First it's Spring, then it's Summer and then we've got Indians and frost coming round some corner or other. It doesn't make any sense at all.'

The truth was that everyone was busy and happy except for Valletta and that made her even **crosser**.

'I want to **do things** again. This isn't **fair.**' Valletta kicked the leg of the table so hard that Oslo's pencil flew out of his paw. What was worse was that she hurt herself. Valletta stomped off with a new pain in her left back paw.

Valletta's cousin Nancy lived in a house under the floorboards of the humans' kitchen with her father, Arran and her uncle, Guernsey. When Valletta poked her head round the door, Guernsey was sitting beside his niece at their kitchen table. In front of them there was a pile of tiny pieces of paper. Guernsey had collected these from human newspapers and he had cut out the letters carefully. They spelt out N-A-N-C-Y

S-T-O-W-A-W-A-Y – Nancy's name. Guernsey slowly pointed out each letter to her, and said the sounds. Then she said them again, copying the way he said them.

'Nuh, Cuh, Yuh – so what do you think these letters say?' Nancy looked at her uncle and smiled. She didn't see what he meant but she was having a nice time with him anyway. She liked this game. Uncle Guernsey was what Great Auntie Sofia called 'a dark horse'.

'That Guernsey, he has hidden depths,' she said, 'and what is more, he reads very, very well.' Great Auntie Sofia couldn't read at all but she could sing and she could knit. Valletta walked up behind Nancy and Guernsey. They didn't seem to notice her at all. This made her even more disgruntled.

'It says N-A-N-C-Y, Nancy,' said Uncle Guernsey. Nancy smiled at him again. 'So what about these letters then dear? Suh, Tuh, Oh – say them after me… what do you think this long word spells?'

'It's Stowaway, you silly mouse,' shouted Valletta. 'It's your whole name - Nancy Stowaway.'

Then, because neither of the other mice said anything back to her, she muddled up all the letters on the table, and ran off.

When Valletta climbed upstairs to the third mousehouse, where her cousins lived with their parents, she found Malaga and Sark playing with Sark's favourite toy. This was a ball made for him, by one of the grown-ups, from the rubber on the end of a pencil. Valletta joined in for a while, but really she wanted Malaga to herself. She wasn't in the patient sort of mood you needed to be in to play with a little boy mouse. Sark was really just a toddler.

Valletta thought for a moment about doing something mean to Sark. And then stopped. She would visit Great Uncle Leningrad and Great Auntie Sofia instead. Finally, someone would take some notice of her!

Chapter 3: Valletta and the Precious Map

Florence smiled at Valletta from her easel in the corner. Great Auntie Sofia put down her knitting, poured Valletta some juice in an acorn beaker and gave her a handful of biscuit crumbs.

'Why don't you sit down, dear? Let's do something together.'

'Knitting,' said Valletta. 'You can teach me to knit.'

'That's a good idea Valletta. Knitting is a good thing to do. If you know how to knit, you can make useful things, and you will never ever be bored.'

Valletta's face began to relax and to unknot itself. She knew Great Auntie Sofia would understand and be kind to her.

'But,' said the older mouse, 'this is not the right day. You won't have enough patience today. You'll make mistakes and then you'll lose interest. We won't be having your first knitting lesson today.'

'Oh please, please. I've got lots of patience. I have.

I have.'

Great Auntie Sofia looked at Valletta and said. 'I promise I'll teach you to knit another day, but today we're going to do something different. We're going to look at the map and we're going to find your place name.'

Aunt Florence, the artist mouse, left her easel in the corner of the room and went to collect the map. When she returned she had a large roll of paper clutched to her furry chest. Very carefully, Florence and Sofia unrolled it and stretched it out on the kitchen table. Valletta fetched beakers and spoons to hold the corners of the paper flat.

All three mice looked at the map.

The paper was crinkly and wrinkly. It was very old. Florence painted in all the outlines whenever they began to fade. There were tiny pawprints next to every place in the world that Valletta's adventurous family had been to. Florence painted the pawprints with ink made of marmite or jam.

All adventures had stopped for a while. Florence noticed that even some of the pawprints were starting to fade. She needed to spend a bright morning checking on them all.

'There's Florence, the place called Florence.' Great Auntie Sofia pointed to two tiny pawprints next to a blob on the map. 'That's our adventure – Grad's and mine. We went there on our honeymoon.' She smiled.

'And there's Sofia,' she moved her paw up the map. Valletta loved the map. She stopped thinking for a little while about where she wasn't going and where she couldn't go. Instead, she started to think about all the stories behind every pawprint. All of the tales that she and all her cousins could look forward to. Tales were told at Moustory Nights every full moon at 46 Spring Blossom Road.

'If there's a good story for every pawprint, then that's an awful lot of stories,' said Valletta.

'You're quite right,' said Great Auntie Sofia. 'You have lots to look forward to.'

Then they all spoke together:

'Are you ready to share and hear the tall tales and long tales and short tales and furry tales, the true tales and very-nearly-true tales about our ancestors, about things that

happened ages and ages ago, and things that happened just a little while ago?'

Valletta's whiskers were beginning to feel that they were pointing the right way again. They were feeling smoother and softer, and more like her whiskers. Her mouth and cheeks weren't feeling tight and itchy any more. She was even starting to forget about the sore paw, from kicking the kitchen table leg.

'Now me,' she said. 'Now my place, Valletta.'

Her aunt and her great aunt looked at the map and moved their paws down the paper. They left the land and skimmed across the blue. Aunt Florence had even painted a couple of tiny dolphins playing and jumping beside a boat.

'This is the Mediterranean Sea,' said Florence. 'All this blue bit, that's what it's called. And here you are, Valletta, on a little island called Malta.'

Valletta stared and stared and was disappointed. 'But there's no pawprint. Why isn't there a pawprint?' For a moment it felt like all the prickles and itches and aches and soreness and **crossness** were coming back.

'It's not fair,' she said again. 'I don't have a pawprint.'

Aunt Florence and Great Auntie Sofia looked at her and smiled. 'That's because a very important mouse didn't go to Valletta. He came from Valletta,' said Sofia.

'And it was his daughter who married your grandfather, and they had a son, who is your father, our Bergie. And he married your lovely mother, Vienna. And they had two mouse children – you and Oslo.'

Valletta, who was already happier than she had been half a minute ago, leaned forwards and rested her chin on her paws. 'What was his name, the mouse who came from Valletta in Malta?' She loved hearing about all the mice who had gone before her.

'Rabat,' Sofia said. 'Rabat was your great-grandfather's name. He was the father of your dear grandmother Casablanca. He brought her to England. I do miss her so.' Her eyes became cloudy for a moment and she wiped them with the back of her paw.

'Will there be a tale about them too?' asked Valletta. 'Because they did travel a very long way, and grandma Casablanca did join our family.'

'Of course, dear,' said Sofia. 'I'll put their tale on Leningrad's list for a Moustory Night.'

Valletta was feeling more like herself again. Great Auntie Sofia drifted off to find her knitting, but Florence stayed and taught Valletta how to mix the inks for map painting.

'You're a quick learner,' she said. 'Maybe next time you can help me with painting over the paws.'

This sounded like a very good idea to Valletta. She sat at the far end of the table and drew little pawprints all over the piece of paper Florence had just given her. It was a bright, sunny morning, so Florence was going to do a little map work while the weather was so nice. The two mice, aunt and niece, sat side by side until lunchtime, and then they carefully lifted the map and hung it over the easel in the corner for the ink to dry.

'We don't want any splots or smudges,' said Florence.

Then Great Auntie Sofia made soup for all three of them, or rather four, as Great Uncle Leningrad turned up from doing something. He sat down and hung his glasses over his right ear, so they didn't mist up while he was eating.

'Valletta is joining us dear,' said Great Auntie Sofia. 'She was having a bit of a sad morning, what with not being able to do the things she likes to do.'

'It's called cabin fever,' said the old mouse, 'when you get fed up with not going adventuring. Are you feeling better now?'

'Oh yes,' said Valletta, 'and I've got a request. A tale. For you to remember and practise for a Moustory Night.'

'You can talk to me about it after lunch when I walk you home,' said Great Uncle Leningrad. They all picked up their spoons and made the loudest, slurpiest, soup-guzzling mouse noises you could ever imagine.

JAM

Chapter 4
Moustory Night

Sark Stowaway, the smallest, plumpest mouse, was playing football. Actually, what he was doing was sometimes throwing his ball and sometimes kicking it. And hoping that someone would throw it back to him or kick it back to him. He didn't mind which.

Sark's ball was made from the rubber from the end of a pencil. A human child must have dropped the pencil through a gap in the floorboards. One of Sark's uncles, Bergen, was very good at making things. As soon as he'd seen the pencil, he rubbed his whiskers and said, 'I know at least one little mouse who will have lots of fun with this.'

The other grown-up mice just let him **get on with it**. Getting on with it meant having a good idea, or more than one good idea, then doing something to **make** that idea happen. So Uncle Bergen had looked at the enormous pencil and had seen, in his imagination, the pencil becoming useful mouse-sized furniture. And mouse-sized picture frames. And the rubbery end of the pencil becoming a football, a toy for his children, his nieces and his little nephew.

Below the floorboards at 46 Spring Blossom Road, everything the mice found was useful. Humans were really very careless with their possessions. They dropped lots on the floor. Sometimes they dropped crumbs of food and sometimes they dropped exciting stuff, like the pencil. Whatever rolled and fell into a gap between the floorboards would be used and treasured by the mice.

On this particular warm morning it was Sark's sister Malaga and his cousin Nancy who were sort of playing with him. Sort of. Because they were also chatting to each other.

'Be kind,' Sark's mum had said to the two girl mice. 'He's younger than you and he needs someone to play with.' Malaga had started to give her mum a why-does-it-have-to-be-me look and then she stopped.

Annécy saw the look anyway. 'Because I'm busy,' she said, 'tidying up, you know, before our visitors arrive. And because you and Nancy know what Sark

gets like.'

Sark was the youngest mouse in the Stowaway family. He lived under the floorboards below the grown-up humans' bedroom with his big sister, Malaga, and with his mother and father. His mother's name was Annécy and his father's name was Jersey. Sark was, his Great Auntie Sofia said, 'a bit of a terror.' When Sark was happy, he chatted and laughed and everybody loved him. He had a giggle which could almost melt cheese. When Sark was not happy, all the mice knew it. His squeak became a screech, and his screech was the loudest screech you could ever imagine. Did this matter? Well, yes it did, because if you were a mouse living under the floorboards of a human house, you would **not** want the humans to hear you.

'Who's visiting?' asked Nancy, for the fourth time.

'You know,' said Malaga, who was quite good at throwing and kicking the ball, and very patient with her cousin as well. 'It's the whole family. It's our turn for Moustory Night.'

Everyone loved Moustory Night. It happened every full moon, when the night was bright and the night was light, and it happened in a different mousehouse each time.

There were four mousehouses at 46 Spring Blossom Road. Next to Sark and Malaga's house was the house where Great Uncle Leningrad lived with Great Auntie Sofia and their beautiful artist daughter, Florence, the youngest of their children. This house was the grandest of all of them. A huge map of the world was stretched out on the floor next to Leningrad, Sofia and Florence's house, because it needed to be kept flat and as uncrinkled as it could be. This map was the most precious thing which the Stowaway family owned. It was special and it was important, and every place they had been to was marked on it with a painted pawprint.

Below the houses belonging to Sark's family and Great Uncle Leningrad's family, there were two more mousehouses. Sark and Malaga's cousin Nancy and her dad Arran lived in one of the downstairs mousehouses, with Arran's younger brother, Guernsey. Nancy didn't have a mother any more, which was very sad. The other mousehouse belonged to two more young mice, Oslo and Valletta, and their parents.

'Tell me about Moustory Night, Malaga,' Nancy said. Nancy was the only one of the three little girl mouse cousins who liked bows and ribbons and soft, fluffy things. She also liked food and playing with her cousins and well, everything really.

'Nancy,' said Great Auntie Sofia, 'is a sunny child. All her squeaks are happy ones, and she tries her best.' Great Auntie Sofia was right of course. Nancy knew perfectly well what Moustory Night was, but she was the kind of mouse who liked things to be explained to her again and again.

'Moustory Night,' said Malaga, after she'd returned the ball to Sark, 'is when we Stowaway mice spend an evening together, once every full moon, and we sing our Stowaway song and all the grown-ups tell our family stories.'

'Tall tales and long tales and short tales and furry tales. True tales and very-nearly-true tales about our ancestors, about things that happened ages and ages ago, and things that happened just a little while ago,' Valletta went on. She'd just arrived to see what was happening.

'I love Moustory Night,' said Nancy. 'I can't wait.'

'Neither can we!' said Valletta and Malaga.

The time between then and the start of Moustory Night passed quite quickly. First, there was the game to finish with Sark, and then the mice separated and went to their own houses for lunch. Afterwards, all five cousins met back at Malaga and Sark's, where they did drawing and colouring for a while. Oslo, the only other boy mouse, drew a couple of pictures for Sark to colour in.

'What a good mouse you are, Oslo!' said his aunt Annécy, who was still **getting things** ready. Oslo felt a bit prickly and twitchy. The three girl mice – his sister Valletta and his cousins, Malaga and Nancy – all poked out their tongues at him and made rude faces. Actually, it was Valletta who started this, but the other two joined in very quickly.

After the drawing and colouring, all five mice had drinks in their acorn beakers and some biscuit crumbs. Then Sark dozed off, clutching his football, and the four older mouse children all helped Annécy with **getting things ready**.

There were chairs to put in rows and plates, cups, bowls and spoons to be arranged on the big table. The table would soon be covered with food. A mouse feast. Everyone coming to the Moustory Night would bring something for all the mice to share. Each of these evenings always began with food.

'We're the Stowaways, the Stowaways;
we like to travel, to go away.
We creep into their bags and cases
and then we visit lovely places.
We can go by car, or go by bus;
all kinds of boats are fine with us,
and if our humans ride by train,

we little mice do not complain.
Just beware if they talk of flights!
Those metal birds give mice a fright!'

This rhyme was the one the mice always sang or spoke at Moustory Night. First, they ate until their tummies were full and then Great Auntie Sofia would either start to sing or speak their Stowaway family rhyme. If she started singing it in her lovely clear singing voice, all the mice sang with her. If she started speaking it, then they all joined in and squeaked it together too.

'Now are your bellies filled, my mouse family?' asked Great Uncle Leningrad.

'Are you ready to share and hear the tall tales and long tales and short tales and furry tales, the true tales and very-nearly-true tales about our ancestors, about things that happened ages and ages ago, and things that happened just a little while ago?'

'YES, YES,' the other mice all said, as they said every time.

And so it began.

Chapter 5
The Tale of Düsseldorf and Alberta

The big table was at the back of the room. Most of the food was gone now and there were piles of dirty plates, cups, bowls and spoons. Behind the table, on the wall, there were lots of pictures. Pictures in frames made from the pencil and other finds. These were pictures of Stowaways, some still remembered and some only remembered through the stories told on Moustory Nights.

Florence the artist mouse had painted some of these portraits. Others had been painted by artist mice who had lived long before her.

In front of the table were two rows of chairs for the adults and for Oslo and Valletta. In front of the chairs the three youngest mice, Sark, Nancy and Malaga, lay on the floor on their full, fat tummies with their back legs out behind them and their little furry chins resting on their front paws. They lay on a soft multi-coloured rug knitted by Great Auntie Sofia. As well as singing, knitting was something she was **very good at**.

Great Uncle Leningrad polished his glasses on his furry stomach and smoothed his long whiskers. He had a little cough and cleared his throat.

'This is a tale and it's a true tale and a short tale and a furry tale. It's about my great, great grandfather Düsseldorf and my great, great grandmother Alberta, when they lived at 46 Spring Blossom Road, and a **cat** came to stay. The reasons for this cat visitor's arrival are lost in history.

Some mice have said the human owners of the house were looking after the cat while its human was in hospital. Other mice have said the cat was a stray with no home. This cannot be true. The cat was large and black and had a mean face. It looked much too well-fed to be a stray. Whatever the reason for it being at 46 Spring Blossom Road, it stayed for three long weeks, and the mice living below the floorboards grew hungrier and hungrier.

Whenever the cat wasn't sleeping, he prowled round and round the kitchen. He found all the little nooks and cracks, holes and gaps from where the mice used to pop out for foraging. The mice couldn't creep out any more. They couldn't sneak out any more.

No scraps.

No crusts.

No crumbs.

No tasty titbits.

What were the mice going to do? How could they feed their hungry family, all living under the floorboards? All with rumbly, grumbly tummies.

And then brave Düsseldorf and brave Alberta hatched a cunning plan. Alberta would distract the cat, draw his attention to her while her husband Düsseldorf made a dash for food. They didn't tell the other mice.

'Too dangerous,' they would be sure to squeak. So Alberta and Düsseldorf whispered their secret plans only to each other.

One dark night, when all the other mice were curled up sleeping and dreaming their twitchy, whiskery dreams, Alberta dashed out of the largest hole in the kitchen, across the floor and up onto the table. She almost slipped as she jumped onto the table top. She couldn't stop herself from making a tiny squeak. The cat woke at once and ran to the table, where he stood on his hind legs and made deep, rumbling sounds. Alberta was only just beyond the reach of a huge black paw with long sharp claws. She knew it was **now or never**. She knew Düsseldorf was collecting food, running back to the hole and pushing it through with all of his strength, as fast as he could, and then running back to collect more.

Alberta sang and danced and twirled as if her life depended on it. Which it did. Her life and Düsseldorf's life depended on her singing, dancing and twirling and **keeping the cat busy** watching her.

At last she heard a small squeak from the other side of the kitchen. The cat's head turned. Alberta ran as fast as she had ever run in her life to the safety of the mousehole. Düsseldorf guarded the hole until his beloved wife was safe inside. But the huge black paw with the long sharp claws reached into the hole and stabbed Düsseldorf. A deep scratch along the whole length of one of his hind legs. He squealed out in pain. Düsseldorf was injured. For ever afterwards, until the end of his mousey life, his leg would be sore and he would limp. But Düsseldorf and Alberta had managed to collect enough food to last the mouse family until the big black cat went home. They had saved their family from starvation.

'Hooray for the brave food-finder Düsseldorf! Hooray for the brave singing and dancing Alberta!' the Stowaways shouted and whooped and cheered and whistled.

Every winter when it was cold, Düsseldorf's old wound ached and Alberta sang soothing songs to distract her brave husband from the pain. And this story was passed down, and it is true, and this is the tale I've told to you.'

Great Uncle Leningrad took off his glasses and wiped his eyes and his audience stamped and clapped.

'I love Moustory Night,' said Nancy.

Chapter 6
Valletta and a Frosty Morning

It was getting colder. Over the four weeks since the last Moustory Night, the little mice were finding it so much harder to get out of their warm beds in the mornings. It was cosy and warm under the covers, but, when their paws touched the floor, that was a different story. Their rubbed their front paws together and sometimes, when they spoke, their breath made wispy patterns in the air.

Great Auntie Sofia and her daughter-in-law, Annécy, were busy knitting bedsocks and bobble hats for all of the Stowaway family. Florence and her cousin's wife, Vienna, joined in too by helping the children make woolly pompoms using circles of cardboard with holes cut out of the middle.

'Woolly pompom making is a good activity for little mice,' said Great Auntie Sofia. 'They can be sewn onto bobble hats, and tea-cosies, and you can make pompoms in cheerful colours for hanging on

Christmouse trees. And wrapping the wool round and through, round and through, is a lovely kind of mousey busyness for chilly afternoons. And when another pompom is finished, it'll be just the right time for hot chocolate and warm scones again.'

One cold morning, Vienna Stowaway stepped out of bed onto the floor and let out a little squeak. 'Bergie, come quickly, the floor's wet.'

Bergen walked round to his wife's side of the bed, bent down and touched the floor. 'Damp, my angel,' he said. 'It's definitely damp.'

Before the two mice thought about breakfast they pushed, and shoved and pulled their bed away from the wall. 'It will be better with an airgap,' said Bergen. The pawmade bed was very heavy, and the noise woke up Oslo, who rushed to help his parents.

'Does your floor feel damp?' said his mother.

'No, but the wall does a little bit,' said Oslo. 'Is it something to do with how cold it is?'

'Hmm,' said Bergen. 'I'm not sure about that.' He

was the kind of father mouse who liked to understand things. He like to know why things were happening.

All three of them stood still when they heard a thump and a squeal.

'MUMMY! DADDY! OSLO!'

'Oh,' said Oslo. 'Valletta's awake then. Guess she's fallen out of bed again.' Valletta fell out of bed quite often. She also shouted a lot. Oslo, her brother, was used to both of these things.

Valletta came running in to join the rest of her family.

'I'm freezing, and my feet are wet **and my bedcover's wet too**.' Now Valletta had a little, but very heavy, pawmade bed which was pushed right up against the wall. Her parents had arranged it like this because she had always been a fidgety mouse, tossing and turning in her sleep.

'At least she'll only have one side of the bed to fall out of,' her father had said. Valletta wasn't just making a fuss this time. Her floor was wet and her bedcover, where it had touched the wall, was a tiny bit wet too.

Now, we're not talking big puddles, or water running down the wall like a stream. But something was **not right at all**.

The four mice pulled Valletta's bed a mousewidth away from the wall and then her mother, Vienna, hung the bedcover over the end of the bed to dry and air it.

After breakfast, Bergen set off to see his cousins, Jersey, Arran and Guernsey. He wanted to hear their thoughts on this new damp wall and floor problem. Arran and Guernsey seemed to have a problem too. They shared a house with Arran's daughter Nancy. But Jersey just shrugged his mousey shoulders and said all was perfectly fine in his house – there was no problem. He, and his wife Annécy, and their children, Malaga and Sark, did not have wet feet, or wet bedcovers or wet walls.

'I think,' said Bergen, 'we should go and see Leningrad and talk to him about it.' And so they did – Bergen, Jersey, Guernsey and Arran – all together.

When these four mice reached the biggest and grandest of the four mousehouses at 46 Spring

Blossom Road, their visit became a meeting.

'Come in dears,' said Great Auntie Sofia. 'I've just brewed a pot of tea.' And so she had. There was a large pot of tea in the middle of the kitchen table with a new knitted cosy on it. On the top of the cosy were two little pompoms made by the mouse children.

'This won't go very far,' said Florence, tucking her paintbrush behind her ear. There were already seven thirsty mice in the kitchen and who knew how many others might arrive? So Florence scampered about finding where Sofia had hidden the second best teapot, and made another pot of tea, just in case.

'We have no problems here,' said Leningrad. This was just as well, because the mouse family's most important treasure was kept next to Leningrad, Sofia and Florence's house. This treasure, of course, was the map.

'It would be dreadful if something happened to damage our map,' said Florence, who was now chewing the end of her paintbrush.

'It seems,' said Leningrad, 'that we are safe here upstairs. The problem is downstairs.'

'Then,' said his nephew Bergen, 'I think the problem is from next door. I suggest that Arran, Guernsey, Jersey and I find out what's going on. We will go to the human house next door and we will report back.'

Great Auntie Sofia thought this was a splendid idea and that, as it was her turn – her and Leningrad and Florence's turn – to have Moustory Night at their house that night, the reporting back would be there and then, that evening. Because the whole family would be gathered together anyway.

'But for now', said Sofia, 'you must pop downstairs, Florence dear, and bring Nancy up to sit with us. Otherwise she'll be on her own while the men mice are discovering what's what.'

The day rolled on. Valletta's bedcover dried and Valletta and her brother helped make soup, peppermint creams and gingerbread men. Their cousin Nancy, who loved food, drifted downstairs to help her cousins and her aunt with all this yumminess.

Sark and Malaga, the other two cousins, were

helping their mother make cheese straws and fruit crumble. And of course they played as well. Sark soon wanted to be rushing about again. Malaga threw a ball for him for a while and then he seemed to want 'piggybacks' for the rest of the afternoon.

The four grown-up mice, the three brothers and their cousin, were gone for a long time. On their way home they visited Great Uncle Leningrad once more. They were cold and their fur was wet. They looked tired as they told Leningrad, Sofia and Florence their terrible news.

'Oh my dear boys,' said Leningrad, shaking his head. 'I think it's far too late to cancel Moustory Night now, but this is not the night we were expecting, and not at all the night we wanted to have.' He gave a long, sad sigh. Then the four other mice went back to their houses to get warm, dry and ready for the evening.

Chapter 7
Stowaways to the Rescue

It was the night of the full moon, the night when all the Stowaway mouse family met together and shared their food, and news, and rhymes and stories. The table in Great Uncle Leningrad and Great Auntie Sofia's kitchen was piled high with deliciousness. All the mice had brought something to share. Soups, pies, puddings and gingerbread men and peppermint creams. There was juice, wine and acorn beer. It looked like a huge feast but Great Auntie Sofia knew most of it would be gone very quickly. Fourteen mice, nine adults and five children, could eat an enormous amount.

The mice ate quickly and then just as everyone was settling into their usual places, Great Auntie Sofia wiped her mouth with a paw, cleared her throat and began to say the Stowaway rhyme:

'We're the Stowaways, the Stowaways;
we like to travel, to go away.

We creep into their bags and cases
and then we visit lovely places.
We can go by car, or go by bus;
all kinds of boats are fine with us,
and if our humans ride by train,
we little mice do not complain.
Just beware if they talk of flights!
Those metal birds give mice a fright!

Early in the lockdown, a couple of the grown-up mice had suggested that they should stop the saying or singing of the Stowaway rhyme, until after it was all over and things got back to normal.

'No,' said Guernsey, who often seemed a bit uncomfortable when he was talking to the whole family. He was happier squeaking to just one or two of his mousey relations at a time. 'Of course we carry on with it. This is our history and it tells us who we are. A few months, or even a year or so, **won't change that**.'

'Hooray for Uncle Guernsey,' said Valletta, who was a very loyal little mouse and a very proud Stowaway.

Everyone agreed with Guernsey and Valletta, and so the usual ways carried on, even in those unusual times.

'Now are your bellies filled, my mouse family?' asked Great Uncle Leningrad. *'Are you ready to share and hear the tall tales and long tales and short tales and furry tales, the true tales and very-nearly-true tales about our ancestors, about things that happened ages and ages ago, and things that happened just a little while ago?'*

'YES, YES,' the other mice all said, as they said every time.

Great Uncle Leningrad smiled at the other thirteen members of his family, from Sofia, his beloved wife, to Sark, his youngest grandchild, and everyone in-between.

'My family,' he said. 'The tale I am telling is a true tale and a sad tale and a now tale. This is no story. This is why the walls, floors and bedcovers have been wet today. There has been a **terrible accident**.'

Some of the mice knew what he was going to say; most of them didn't. All of them sighed and smoothed their whiskers.

'Our humans' house, at 46 Spring Blossom Road, is what is called a semi-detached house. It is joined on to its neighbour, 48 Spring Blossom Road.' The children looked puzzled. The adult mice arranged their tails across their laps or around the legs of their chairs.

'At 48 Spring Blossom Road, on the ground floor, a pipe has burst and water has poured everywhere. Some of you may know that the upstairs at Number 48 has been modernised. There are new floorboards with no gaps and there are 'fitted carpets.' It is not an upstairs where mice can live anymore.'

Great Uncle Leningrad shook his head and his audience, even the little ones who didn't really understand, shook their heads too.

'And so, my dears, at Number 48, all of the mice – our neighbours but not our family – live downstairs. And downstairs there is more water than any of us have ever seen. It is a flood.

Some of you will know that there are two mice families who live downstairs, Mr and Mrs Longears and their thirteen children, nieces and nephews, and one other family, Mr and Mrs Tunefully and their much smaller family of two children. We have seen Gertrude Longears today. She and her family have had to leave their flooded home . But they are all safe. They have moved to the garage. It is not perfect, no, not at all. But they are alive and well and happy to be so.

My tale, my dear, dear Stowaway mice, is about the Tunefullys. None of us has ever met any of these neighbours, the Tunefullys, before. All we know is that they are a musical family and an adventurous family, but I am not going to tell you about an adventure. I have news, such sad news, to tell you about them.'

Leningrad's family was quiet and still. They had a feeling that they were going to hear something very bad.

'We never met them, my dears, but Gertrude Longears told us today that the Tunefully family came from the North. They escaped from a flooded house and made their way down to the South where we are, for a new life. It is a flood again which has caused this dreadfulness. Tragically, Mr and Mrs Tunefully drowned today, and they have left behind a young lady mouse and a half-grown son. These two have no home and no parents.'

There was a shocked gasp from the crowd.

'Where are the poor dears now?' asked Vienna, who was a kind mouse and a caring mother.

'For tonight, they are with the Longears family in the garage. But this cannot continue. I am suggesting to you all, my family, that we must help. We Stowaways must offer a home to the Tunefully orphans.'

'Oh my goodness,' said Annécy, who did not like change very much. 'Where will we put them?'

'We will find a way,' said Great Uncle Leningrad. 'We will find a way and we will make a plan. And we will do it soon and we will meet again after breakfast. Now there are things to think and things to do and we all need sleep. Goodnight Stowaways.'

The mice realised that Leningrad was telling them all to go home. This was not a happy Moustory Night, the sort of Moustory Night they were used to. The mice were filled with confused and sad thoughts.

'I won't,' said Annécy, 'get a wink of sleep tonight.' She and her husband Jersey had just tucked Malaga and Sark up in bed and given each of them a tickly kiss on the cheek. Annécy was now sitting up in her bed with a cup of warm camomile tea in one paw. The other paw was busy twirling the ends of her whiskers round and round. She was frowning too.

'You'll go out like a light, darling, just as soon as you get that camomile tea down. What we all need, after news like this, is a good night's sleep.' Her husband was talking in a very quiet soothing voice, as he could see how bothered she was. Secretly, he was more than a bit worried too. Did they really have to look after two strangers, two mice from next door? They'd never met them. It was hard enough keeping all fourteen Stowaways – the whole family who lived at Number 46 – safe and well-fed. Without having two new mouths to feed. Two new mice to keep safe.

'Oh dear,' said Jersey to himself. He knew his wife very well. She worried about any change, or anything which could bring danger to the family. But, as soon as her velvety ears touched the pillow, she slept. Always. Whatever the problem was.

Jersey lay in the dark for a while, fretting about the next day. What were they going to do?

In every mousehouse under the floorboards at 46 Spring Blossom Road, at least one of the mice who lived there lay awake for some time. And, in each house, the mouse left awake scratched his or her ears, twirled his or her whiskers or chewed the thin skin on the inside of his or her cheek. Because there was a lot to think about.

There had nearly been three quarters of a year since all the strangeness started. That's three quarters of a year of not being able to go to the places they usually went to. Or do the things they usually did. Or jump into

a handbag,

or a laptop case,

or a school bag,

or a shopping bag,

or a rucksack,

or a case

whenever the humans went out and about or around or away. For an hour, or half a day. Or a whole day. Or a holiday. The humans weren't actually going anywhere any more. Just a quick trip to the supermarket, or a little walk round the park, or sitting out in the garden when the weather was nice. There was just that one holiday to the countryside in August. And there was the **Fursday** evening clapping and banging of saucepans and stuff.

Apart from these things, there had been nothing. The humans were there at home. All of the time. And that made life very hard for the mouse family. Foraging was so much riskier. And just as the family of humans got bored or fed up or cross sometimes, so too did the families of mice under the floorboards.

Not all mouse families like trips and travels, journeys and outings. But some do. And the Stowaway family were famous for their adventures.

'Oh dear,' said Jersey Stowaway to himself again.

His wife was now snoring in a snufflywifflywhistly mousey sort of way and he didn't want to wake her. 'I suppose the others have thought of a **plan**. But I haven't.'

By midnight even the most anxious mice were asleep, twitching their velvety ears and noses and there was snufflywifflywhistly snoring coming from all four mousehouses.

1
2
3

Chapter 8
Getting Ready for the Tunefullys

'We don't have a choice,' said Great Uncle Leningrad. He thumped the kitchen table and his glasses jumped up in the air and settled down again, further down towards the tip of his nose. 'We must help our brother mice. They need us.'

'But they're not my brothers,' said Malaga. 'I've only got one brother, and he's quite enough. I don't want any more.' Then she frowned, crossed her paws and looked very hard at the table.

The grown-up mice all stared at her. Great Auntie Sofia looked surprised, because it was generally Valletta who could be relied on to speak her mind. Not Malaga.

Later that morning, nearly all of the children were drawing and colouring at Bergen and Vienna's house.

'I know Malaga can be led astray, but she's a good little mouse at heart,' Great Auntie Sofia said to Annécy and Florence. 'I was surprised that she wasn't kinder.'

'Great Auntie Sofia,' said Valletta, who was not happy at what had been said. 'Malaga wasn't being unkind. She doesn't know any nearly grown children – she must think having this new boy around will be like having another little Sark. Football, and piggybacks, and temper tantrums.'

'You're right, my dear,' said Sofia. 'The children probably weren't listening, or were getting tired, when my Leningrad got to the part about how old the Tunefully children are.'

'How old are they exactly?' asked Annécy. Her sleep had done her a lot of good. Today, she'd woken up feeling very different. Sort of whatever'ish. But not in a rude or grumpy way. More in a 'whatever-happens-is-going-to-happen-and-we'll-make-the-best-of-it' sort of way.

'We don't quite know yet,' said Sofia. 'But the girl is almost grown up, I believe. And they're much older than any of our little ones.'

'They'll be a help,' said Florence, who tended to look on the bright side. 'Not a burden to us.'

'First, we must let them feel sad, and cry if they need to.' Sofia said. 'They've had a terrible shock.'

The first part of the **plan** happened straight after breakfast and after the meeting. Bergen and Arran were chosen to go next door and speak to Mr and Mrs Longears, and to meet the two Tunefullys.

Great Uncle Leningrad chose Bergen and Arran because 'Bergie is practical and sensible,' he said, and then he paused, 'and Arran understands about sad things. And will show sympathy.'

Of course, this was a good choice. Bergen was good at deciding things, and thinking 'on his paws.' Arran did understand about sad things. Very sad things. His beloved Shannon, Nancy's mother, had died two winters ago.

Because it was daytime, the visit was risky. The two grown-up mice squeezed out through the airbrick at the front of the kitchen, scampered all the way to the far end of Number 48 Spring Blossom Road and slid under the garage door, which didn't reach quite down to the ground. They told Mr and Mrs Longears that they would come back that evening, under the cover of darkness, and collect the two Tunefullys.

Mrs Gertrude Longears clapped her paws together and then hugged both Bergen and Arran one at a time.

'We are so grateful, my dears,' she said. 'We've been worrying dreadfully about how to feed two more. We do want to help, but it's just so difficult, what with the move, and the drying of things, and having to make a new home.' Mrs Longears was smiling but her lip was trembling, and her eyes had filled with tears.

The two young Tunefullys were still too shocked and too damp and too sad to do any thanking or hugging. They just nodded when Bergen told them they'd have a new home next door and that he and Arran would collect them as soon as it got dark.

'What did they say?' asked Leningrad, when Bergen and Arran returned. Florence, Sofia and Annécy were drinking tea at the far end of the table but Sofia had got out her knitting bag and was murmuring about warm bedsocks for the new arrivals.

Bergen told them how thankful Mr and Mrs Longears were.

'But Uncle, we need to make the holes in the airbricks larger,' said Bergen. 'Arran will help me this afternoon. And I'm sure Guernsey will lend a paw too. The Tunefullys will have possessions to bring. The passage will have to be wider.'

'Good idea, my boy, but quietly. You must not be discovered.'

'I'm going to get Oslo to help,' said Bergen. 'He can guard the entrance at this end and help to pull things through with Guernsey and Jersey.'

Great Auntie Sofia dropped her needles and wool and looked up in alarm. 'But he's only a child,' she said.

'He's a brave boy mouse,' said Arran. 'I'm sure Berg's right.'

Bergen and his cousin were on their way out of the door when Arran turned round and said to his father and the three female mice in the room. 'You know this is just the beginning, Dad, us bringing the Tunefully boy and girl to stay with us?'

'What do you mean Arran?' said Florence and Annécy at the same time.

Arran shook his head and scratched his velvety chin. 'We have seen things this morning. Yes, we can help the Tunefullys today. But tomorrow, and the next day, and the day after, we must come up with a plan. We have to help the Longears family too.'

Bergen stopped in the doorway to agree with his cousin. 'The Longears family have lost almost everything. They're trying to dry out what's left, on top of the gas boiler in the garage. They all slept in an old apple box last night. But it's draughty and they don't have a proper safe home yet. There are thirteen Longears children with only two adults. It's a huge job for them. And winter is almost here.'

'We have to help them,' said Arran. 'We'll get the Tunefullys here safely, with whatever we can of their things. You can sort out who's sleeping where…and then tomorrow, the real work begins.'

Arran and Bergen left the room and there was a little silence.

Great Auntie Sofia spoke first. 'Could you fetch a pencil and a piece of paper, Florence dear? I think your father needs to make a list.'

Annécy kissed the two lady mice goodbye and went to check on the children and to sort out lunch.

Florence found a piece of paper and a pencil, and a tiny knife to sharpen the pencil with.

And Great Uncle Leningrad took off his glasses, and wiped them, and put them down on the table. And then he wiped his eyes with a paw, because he said that some specks of dust were making them itch.

'I'm proud of those mice,' he said to his wife. 'They've got good, kind hearts.'

Number one, wrote Florence…

'Sometimes, when an important thing is about to happen – a thing that's a bit scary too – it's much better if everyone keeps busy,' said Florence to her mother. That afternoon, everyone did have something to do. Great Uncle Leningrad started on his organising list after lunch. He would say **number two** or **number**

three or **number twenty-seven** and then think of some words to go after the numbers. And Florence would write them down.

It was like a shopping list, or a list of ingredients for a recipe. Only it was meant to be a list of things for everyone in Leningrad's family to do to get ready for the arrival of the two Tunefullys and for everything that would happen next. But, after Florence had got to the end of writing down **number four**, and the fourth thing to do, she noticed that Leningrad had fallen asleep in his chair. She took his glasses off gently, and hooked them over one of his ears, so he'd know where to find them when he woke up.

Annécy had an afternoon without her children. At lunchtime, Jersey said, 'I'll take the little ones this afternoon, darling. We need to keep them out of the way of all the comings and goings and to-ings and fro-ings at Bergie's place. Until the Tunefullys are here.'

'Good idea,' said Annécy. 'Yes, you keep them here, and I can help with beds and food or something.

There'll be plenty to do.'

Oslo had been invited to join his father and his other two uncles for the afternoon, so the plan was now for Jersey to look after the four younger ones – his own two children, Malaga and Sark, and then Nancy and Valletta too. Jersey's house was upstairs, closest to Leningrad, Sofia and Florence's house. Jersey knew his father tended to have a little nap in the afternoons, so he closed the door. That way, the children wouldn't be able to disturb Leningrad's snoozes.

So Great Uncle Leningrad was dozing, and snoring very loudly. Great Auntie Sofia was knitting two new bobble hats. She was sitting in the chair next to him, with her knitting basket by her hind paws. She was wearing a pair of bedsocks she'd made a week or so earlier. It was starting to get chilly in the afternoons. Winter wasn't coming. It was here already.

Bobble hats - she wasn't sure of the sizes of the Tunefully boy and girl. But she needed to make a start. Later, there would be more bedsocks to do as well.

Back in those days before everything became strange, before the adventures stopped, before no Stowaways could stow away anywhere anymore, whenever Jersey looked after the children, this meant

noisy games,

and boisterous games,

and games that ended with jumping on beds and throwing cushions,

and games where children got very hot and over-excited.

And sometimes one of them would fall and hurt themselves, or pull the tail or whiskers of one of the other children, or break something. There would sometimes be tears, and often be 'staying up too late', or 'eating far too many sweets'. That was the way it went.

So the Stowaway children always loved it when it was Jersey's turn to look after them. Except, perhaps Oslo, who sometimes found his younger sister and his cousins a bit too much.

Of course, shouty games and squealing, shrieking little mice were **just not possible** with the human family being upstairs. So, for this afternoon, Jersey had another plan.

'Oh, lush,' said Malaga. Lush was her new favourite word. Nancy and Sark looked happy. Valletta didn't look unhappy. They were going to make chocolate cake. With icing. And this was for eating, instead of a normal pudding, at supper time that evening. When there would be two extra mice.

Now, all of the mouse children helped in the kitchen and all of the mouse children liked cooking. But with Jersey, it was so much more exciting.

Cooking with Jersey always meant making something messy with lots of ingredients and using lots of stuff. Spoons, knives, jugs, sieves, bowls, whisks, pans, baking tins, scales and cooling trays. Lots of stuff.

Annécy sometimes squeaked privately to Vienna. 'It's so nice that he likes cooking, and he is a marvellous mousterchef. But why, oh why, must he be so messy?'

If Jersey cooked for his family – no surface stayed

unsticky; no pan or bowl was **unused**; the floor was slippery; the walls were splashed and the chairs were powdery. If you were silly enough to put your paws on the table, they stuck to it.

When Annécy walked into Vienna and Bergen's house that afternoon she said, ' Jer's making chocolate cake with the kids.'

'You're brave,' said Vienna.

'Oh well, ' said Annécy, who sounded a bit braver than she felt. 'They'll have a great time. And it's only mess…'

Vienna, Annécy and Florence – who were all great friends, as well as being family – started to work. The first job was to work out where the new arrivals would sleep.

'The boy can share with Oslo in his room,' said Vienna. 'And Nancy's got a spare bed in her room – we'll put the girl in with her.'

'Shouldn't they both be in the same house?' said Florence.

'Too cramped,' said Vienna. 'They should be fine like this – after all, they'll be neighbours.'

And so that's how it was arranged. A bed was made up in Oslo's room, in Vienna and Bergen's house below the humans' living room. This was quite hard for the lady mice to do. Bergen had made all the beds in his house. They were strong and heavy, and much better than the twiggy bedframes which had been there before.

A bed was made up in Nancy's room, in the house she shared with her father, Arran, and her uncle, Guernsey. A little bit more shuffling around had to be done in both homes too. There was furniture to be moved, because the floor in Nancy's house and the floor and wall in Oslo and Valletta's house were all still damp.

The flood next door had been yesterday, but it had started in the night before, when the pipe burst. It seemed like a lot was changing for the Stowaway mice, and it was changing very quickly.

Chapter 9
New Arrivals

Oslo was excited to be with his dad and with two of his uncles. This was much more grown up than spending the afternoon with the other four little mice. Bergen, Arran and Guernsey started looking at the airbrick which led to the outside.

For mice this was a very useful airbrick. Fresh air came in through it and light came in too. On rainy evenings, after the little mice were tucked up in bed, the adult mice would push water containers out through the holes in the brick, and then pull them in again the next morning. On thin, plaited ropes of human hair. Very slowly and gently.

Because, of course, all creatures have to drink. Not to mention the washing up. And sometimes a lick and a paw wipe just wasn't quite enough to deal with grubby young mice.

Now, this airbrick was big enough for an average-sized mouse to squeeze through, but what they didn't know was how much the two Tunefullys would be bringing with them. So it was decided to file through a couple of the bars carefully so they could be put back in place afterwards. And so the humans would never know!

Arran had a human nail-file, which he'd sharpened, and the grown-up mice took it in turns to file neatly through the clay bars, as quietly as possible. From time to time you could hear –

'Oslo, could you just sweep that bit please,' and Oslo would sweep up another pile of reddish dust. After a while, Bergen looked at his young son holding the dustpan and brush, and saw that Oslo wasn't looking quite so keen as he had before. So then, the four mice took it in turns to file and sweep up, even if it was a bit slower that way.

And then they collected all the reddish dust and poured it into a little jar, because mice don't waste things and because Florence, the artist mouse, would be sure to have a good idea for what to do with it.

When the beds and furniture were all sorted out, Annécy and Florence went upstairs to help Sofia make supper for sixteen. Not fourteen this evening. She left Vienna downstairs pouring out acorn beakers of squash for the four dusty male mice.

Not a sound was coming from Jersey and Annécy's kitchen. Florence peeked around the door. Valletta and Jersey were standing next to the freshly iced cake, admiring it. Valletta was sneaking cake crumbs that had fallen through the cooling tray into her paw. Malaga was licking a wooden spoon. Sark had the mixing bowl on his head. Nancy was licking the table and seemed to be covered in cocoa powder.

'Oh darlings,' said Florence. 'What a lovely time you've had. The cake looks brilliant. I'll just pop it next door to Auntie Sofia's so it's ready for after supper, and Valletta will come with me to lay the table.'

Like a flash, Florence delivered both a young helper and a cake next door, stopping first to wipe a little brown mark off Valletta's whiskers and to make sure she'd given her paws a quick lick.

'Valletta's going to help you, Annécy,' said Florence.

'I'll just go and give Jersey a paw with the washing up. Won't be a mo.'

Annécy knew there would be an awful lot of mess in her kitchen and she was very, very grateful that Florence was dealing with it. Annécy was the opposite of her husband. She was a neat and tidy mouse. Sometimes it was easier for her not to see the mess Jersey had made.

So supper was started and Valletta was actually very helpful. Florence went to organise Jersey and the clearing up. And she washed the three small mice as well as she could, what with all the wriggling and the squeaking.

She left Nancy till last. Though not the youngest, Nancy was the stickiest. She was pretty well caked in cake and cake mixture and icing.

'I'm made of cake and I look like cake and I love cake,' said Nancy, and she and Malaga giggled.

Somehow, Florence was able to make some sort of cleaning magic happen. 'You'll do,' she said and led the three youngest next door.

Great Uncle Leningrad woke suddenly. 'Do I smell

cake, my dears?'

'Yes, but it's for later, Daddy,' said Florence. 'Paws off. I'll make you a nice cup of mint tea for now.'

Everyone was in the kitchen, well nearly everyone. Bergen, Oslo, Vienna and Arran were still missing. Jersey had arrived. Guernsey had come upstairs and was now sitting, bouncing Malaga and Sark on his lap. The table was once again full of food.

'What's happening?' said Great Uncle Leningrad. 'Are they here yet?'

'Yes,' said Guernsey. 'We've got the Tunefullys and all the stuff we could rescue. There's a trunk, full of something or other, and a rug and a writing desk. I think everything must be soaked. The rug is anyway. Oh, and there were musical instruments, and a music stand. You know, the sort that folds up.'

Nobody did know what he meant, but they nodded with interest.

'Oh and we've pushed the pieces back in, on the airbrick, but we might need to have another look at it in the morning.'

'But where are they then, our new guests?' asked Sofia. 'Supper is ready now.'

'I'm sure they'll be up soon,' said Guernsey. 'Vienna's just showing them where they're sleeping.'

At that moment, Bergen, Oslo and Arran walked into the room, looking very hungry. Vienna followed them with the half-grown boy Tunefully, and the girl Tunefully standing just behind her. Great Auntie Sofia looked at the boy, who was not very tall, not much taller than Oslo, but thin and very tired looking. The boy didn't say anything.

'This is Kendal,' Vienna said. 'He's staying in Oslo's room.' Oslo must have known this already because he didn't say anything.

'Kendal?' Valletta asked. 'I thought only Stowaways had place names as their names.'

She sounded puzzled and stared hard at both of the strangers. They were both older than her, and taller than her. Great Uncle Leningrad smiled at the boy,

Kendal Tunefully, with his dampish dark fur and a torn cotton scarf around his neck. Then he smiled at Valletta.

'You are right and you are wrong, Valletta. Kendal is a place in the North of the country and Kendal is this boy's name. We are not the only family of mice who give their children the names of places. The Tunefullys have done this too. For a very long time. They were once a travelling family, and they have always been a musical family. And now they are with us.'

'And this is Ireleth,' said Vienna, 'and yes, Ireleth has told me that her name is the name of another place in the North. Ireleth is going to share Nancy's room.'

'NO, NO, NO, I don't want to share.' So now there were two mice children, Valletta and her younger cousin Nancy, who were not happy. This was yet another change in their young lives.

Great Auntie Sofia looked at both of them. In a kind but no-nonsense sort of way. 'You will sit either side of me, Valletta and Nancy, and you won't say another word. Welcome, my dears. Now let's all sit down and eat.'

The two cross mice sat either side of Great Auntie Sofia and ate, looking down at their plates. Everyone else tucked in to their food happily. The two Tunefullys were polite and quiet, and started slowly, but then they realised it wasn't rude to eat and to eat a lot here. They didn't have to hold back as they had at the Longears' table. Here there was enough for everybody.

Most of this family were welcoming, except perhaps two of the little girl mice, but they would soon come round. Kendal and Ireleth were safe at last. They would soon be dry and warm too.

Chapter 10
Ireleth

Valletta and Nancy were really only cross for about ten minutes. Then they stopped looking at their plates, lifted their little mouse faces and started staring at the new arrivals, Kendal and Ireleth Tunefully.

They were not like any mice Valletta and Nancy had ever seen. Yes, they looked a bit dirty, and you could see they hadn't slept well the last night. But there had been a flood, and they had lost their parents. And they had spent time in an apple box, in a damp, cold garage with thirteen little mice and two grown-up mice. Who had been kind to them but…

Valletta and Nancy sort of understood what Kendal and Ireleth had been through. But, despite all the bad events of the last couple of days, the two new mice sitting at Great Uncle Leningrad and Great Auntie Sofia's table had sleek, glossy dark coats with long whiskers and shiny eyes. They looked **extraordinary**.

Kendal winked at Valletta and Nancy, and then there

was another wink for Malaga and Sark. Then he just nodded in Oslo's direction. For Oslo was a slightly older mouse, and could be quite a serious mouse, and maybe a wink wouldn't go down quite so well with him.

Of course, Ireleth noticed that all the little mice were staring at her and her brother. All at once, she lifted one of her long thin dark paws up in the air and slid two brightly coloured bracelets, (made of some sort of tied threads), off her paw and onto the table.

'They're called 'friendship bracelets',' she said to Valletta and Nancy. In a way neither of them had heard a girl mouse squeak before. 'One for you, little mouse, and one for you, not-so-little mouse,' and she slid one onto Nancy's paw, and one onto Valletta's.

By now the other three mouse children were watching in fascination. Next, Ireleth lifted her right hind paw up onto the table. Right there, in the middle of the food, the plates, and the acorn beakers. And cutlery and all the other stuff. She had five or six more of these bright cotton bands around her ankle too.

'One more, for you, little girl mouse,' she said and

skimmed a bracelet, (or anklet), across the table to Malaga. It landed just on the edge of her plate. 'And,' she said, looking straight at Oslo, 'they're not just for girls. Show them, Kendal.'

And her brother obediently lifted his right hind paw onto the table as well, and sort of flicked one of his 'friendship bracelets' in Oslo's direction.

'Here you are,' he said. 'Catch.'

Oslo caught it.

Sark, who was, after all, a very young mouse, saw that presents were being given, or thrown, to his cousins and to his sister. HE didn't have a present. His furry lip wobbled. Ireleth, whose right hind paw was now back where you'd expect it to be, jumped up and stretched right across the table, and pulled Sark, by his arms, from his mother Annécy's lap.

'Are you thinking I've left you out, little mouse?' she said, swinging him high up into the air. 'I'll come up to your house, after breakfast, tomorrow, and you and I are going to make one. Just your size. Just for you.'

Sark smiled and giggled. Ireleth walked round the

table and set him back, gently, on Annécy's lap.

For a moment or two, everyone was still. After all, Stowaway mice did not usually rest their hind paws on the table, or throw or flick things at each other at mealtimes. This was very odd. Then all the 'could you please pass the' and 'can I cut you another slice' and all the other more usual supper chitchat started up again.

Ireleth and Kendal were quiet as, quiet as…mice, for the rest of the meal, except for once, when Kendal flicked a very small piece of bread at Valletta.

'They really do,' said Great Auntie Sofia, (after the clearing the table, and the washing up, and the 'oh do we have tos' and the 'but it's not time yets' and all the goodnight kisses and hugs were done with), 'they **really** do have the most unusual table manners, these young Tunefullys.'

'Indeed they do,' said her husband, who was concentrating on hooking his glasses over the bedhead. And then, after he'd kissed her whiskery, velvety nose he said, 'I think, my dear, that these young people are going to turn out to be **very interesting**.'

But she was already sleeping. Great Uncle Leningrad scratched his ears, let out a big, long sigh and lay in the dark for a while before drifting off.

'Where's Oslo?' Vienna asked, puzzled. It was after breakfast the next day, and everyone else was where they were expected to be, except for Kendal. He was missing too.

Ireleth had kept her promise to Sark. Just now she was sitting on the floor upstairs with Sark and Malaga, making a 'friendship bracelet' which she then slipped over one of Sark's very chubby ankles. Malaga and Sark could not take their eyes off her. She played piggybacks and kicked the ball with both of them, and taught them all the mousey nursery rhymes like 'three blind mice' and 'hickory dickory dock'. And she told them the Cinderella story. In Ireleth's Cinderella story, the heroine was a poor mouse and it was four robins who changed into the coachmen, and a marmalade orange which became a coach....

Jersey found he had a little bit of time to himself, before Ireleth kissed both children and drifted next door to help Annécy and Great Auntie Sofia.

'She's a marvel,' said Jersey to Annécy, that evening, '...brilliant with the kids.'

Ireleth was keen to help next door at Sofia's house too, but not quite so useful there, as it seemed that she had never ever learned to lay a table, or to make a pot of tea.

Great Auntie Sofia thought this was a little strange, although she said, later, that Ireleth sang so well while they worked that it lifted everyone's mood. 'Such a brave young girl, after the tragedy...'

Nancy stayed downstairs, with Valletta and Vienna. She tried to help Vienna a bit, and then sat at the table drawing until lunch. Oslo did not turn up till lunchtime, and when he did, he was dirty and dusty, and seemed tired.

'I think he's been showing Kendal around,' said

Valletta. Secretly she was quite pleased about this. Because Oslo had wandered off, and was busy with Kendal, it meant she was now able to do his job.

'It doesn't matter about Oslo, 'said Valletta. 'I can keep watch and warn you if there's danger.' She could. And she did.

'Good girl, Valletta,' said Great Uncle Leningrad, who was sitting in Bergen and Vienna's kitchen while they were all working on their 'how-to-help-the-Longears-family' plan.

There was a lot of keeping watch to do. Every morning Bergen, (plus Florence and either Arran or Guernsey), would make the dangerous journey out through the airbrick and all the way to the garage at Number 48. This was where the Longears family were now staying since the flood which had wrecked their home and most of their things. Sometimes it was two trips, what with carrying tools, and materials, and elevenses. And then at lunchtime, (later than their usual lunchtime), they had to do the same risky trip back. For most of the next seventeen mornings, it was Valletta, and not Oslo, who was on guard.

Nancy, this morning and every one of the seventeen mornings after, was torn between watching all the goings-on downstairs, and wanting to be wherever the new, almost grown-up, dark, glossy and beautiful mouse – Ireleth – was. For now, Nancy sat on the floor pulling her tail and listening.

Bergen had piled up lots of useful tools on the kitchen table. He was filling up his carpenter's belt with hammers and screwdrivers and such like. Arran and Guernsey were filling up a large bag with bits of wood. They both helped Bergen that first day.

Florence came down with a basket full of two large bottles of squash, some acorn beakers and a wrapped paper bundle of cookies and cakes, gingerbread men and some pretty macaroons ('macarons' as Annécy called them). For these would be the mid-morning snacks for the rescue team next door.

'I'm coming too,' said Florence. 'After all, there isn't any map work to do now, and I can help Mrs Longears with all the little ones.' She also had a good eye for making things look nice, and arranging things, so she was doubly useful. Bergen and Florence were in the working party every morning. Bergen knew how to make and fix stuff, so he was a very useful mouse in a MICIS.

So this was the new plan and the new pattern to the Stowaways' days.

After breakfast, Great Uncle Leningrad went downstairs to his nephew Bergen's house and supervised, until everyone who was going to Number 48 Spring Blossom Road, went. Then Leningrad went back upstairs for the morning while Great Auntie Sofia and her daughter-in-law Annécy made lunch for all Stowaways and Tunefullys – all sixteen of them. Sometimes he played a game of Snap or Snakes and Ladders with Malaga. Sometimes he snoozed.

Sorting out a new warm, dry home for all fifteen of the Longears family was a lot of hard work. 'But we Stowaways like a challenge, and we must help our neighbours in their time of need,' said Great Uncle Leningrad.

No one suggested that Ireleth or Kendal should

help.

'Much too upsetting for the poor dears to go back there yet,' said Great Auntie Sofia. 'They can stay here with us.'

Actually, there was a lot of extra work for Great Auntie Sofia, and Annécy, and Vienna. They were now a family of fourteen plus two visitors. The two extra mice ate as much as the grown-ups, and the working party was always starving when they all came home for lunch. And there was always a little something - a pie or a tart, a cake or a stew, or a big pot of soup – to be taken to the next door neighbours.

So there was more food to find, more food to be cooked, and so much more clearing up to be done than before.

Great Auntie Sofia was **exhausted**.

Valletta's loud clear squeaking voice was well-known to her family. Sark could squeak, shriek, grumble and grizzle like all little toddler mice could, but Valletta's voice was very different. For fifteen days, Valletta's **loud squeaking voice** was not needed. On the sixteenth day, Florence, Bergen, Arran and Guernsey were climbing back through the airbrick outside the humans' kitchen when a mouse-sized screwdriver slipped from Berg's belt and pinged out onto the path.

Valletta was sitting very quietly in one of the airbrick holes, with a pile of cotton threads next to her for making bracelets, anklets, necklaces and things, as she, Oslo, Malaga and Nancy had been taught to do by Ireleth. Valletta saw what happened at once and quivered as she watched Uncle Guernsey rush back to collect the screwdriver without checking all was clear.

It wasn't clear at all. A human was just coming out of the kitchen with a bag of rubbish for the huge metal bin outside the door, (the door leading to the back garden at 46 Spring Blossom Road).

'GUERNSEY, UNCLE GUERNSEY!' She squeaked, making the shrillest, most high-pitched sound, a sound which no human could hear but no mouse could avoid hearing.

Guernsey scooped up the screwdriver and dived behind the dustbin in the nick of time. In his rush not to be seen by the human, he dropped the screwdriver. It hit the dustbin and made a small noise like a bell, the sort you'd hear on a cat collar, or on a goat a very long way away. The human stopped, hearing something, then looked up to the fence and then at the sky.

'I must top up the bird feeder,' said the human, 'and remember to bring out my binoculars. They haven't all migrated south for the winter.' The human couldn't see the bird that he thought had made the tiny bell-like noise, so he shivered and went back inside.

Valletta smiled to herself and then squeaked at Guernsey. 'Now Uncle Guernsey. Quickly.'

He scampered from his hiding place back to the airbrick. He was safe. But it had been a close thing! As he reached Valletta he picked her up in a huge, happy mouse hug. 'You,' he said, 'would have made Alberta Stowaway, your ancestor, very, very proud.'

Chapter 11
The Tunefullys' Trunk

Late that afternoon, just before supper, Bergen and Great Uncle Leningrad were chatting downstairs at Berg's house about the next, and final, couple of days' work.

'Annécy and Vienna are coming tomorrow, Uncle, for the final cleaning and organising. Florence is staying here tomorrow and she says she's working on activity packs, things for all the little Longears to do when we've finished helping them build their new home. Florence wants to make things to help Mrs Longears out, for after we've left . And then Flo will come in on the last day with me and Guernsey.'

'Splendid,' said Great Uncle Leningrad.

At that moment Florence was drawing 13 pictures with complete outlines, (for colouring in), 13 pictures with broken outlines and 13 pictures made out of dots (for joining up and then colouring in). She also made a pile of mazes with a mouse picture on the outside of the maze, and a cheese picture in the middle.

Valletta and Malaga were sorting them out so they could be packed away before supper.

'Will you do some more for us as well?' said Malaga. 'It's not fair if everything's for the Longears children, and not for us!'

'Come on Mal,' said Valletta. 'Auntie Florence is really tired.'

Florence put down her pencil and scratched Malaga between the ears. 'Of course I will, Mal. Tomorrow. I'm here tomorrow. Not tonight. My paws are aching.'

Nancy was on Arran's lap. He was telling her how brave Valletta had been.

'We're nearly done next door. I'm home with you from tomorrow,' said Arran. 'Uncle Guernsey's working at Number 48 for the last two mornings.'

Nancy sighed happily. Everything was different since the flood and the arrival of the Tunefullys.

There were still no real Stowaway adventures, but her family was busier. Much busier. Especially her dad, who seemed happier. He played with her more, and told her stories again. It wasn't just Uncle Guernsey now. And then there was Ireleth. And she, thought Nancy, seemed to be pretty well perfect.

Bergen and Vienna were having a small cup of bramble wine each and sharing an even smaller piece of ginger cake. They were chatting about the day.

'Valletta was fantastic today,' said Berg. 'Her squeaking saved Guernsey.'

Vienna shuddered. She hated to think of any of her family being in danger, but yes, she felt very proud of Valletta.

'She's not been nearly so moody, darling,' she said. 'Why, I wonder? Is it because of Ireleth?'

'I don't know what it is. Ireleth's definitely got a special way with the small ones, with Jer and Annécy's two, and of course, Nancy. I don't think with Valletta quite so much,' said Bergen, scratching his front whiskers.

'Hmmm,' said Vienna. 'Watch this space!' She twitched her nose and whiskers in the way she had when Bergen first had first seen her. It was lovely. She obviously had the tiniest of ideas starting to form in her mousey head. Her husband didn't understand her, but it was nearly bedtime, and he was far too tired to ask.

These things, whatever they were, would happen if they were meant to happen. He fell asleep remembering the twitching nose and whiskers of Vienna.

Now all this is leaping ahead. It had been three weeks since the Tunefullys and Longears plan had begun. The first part had been rescuing Kendal and Ireleth Tunefully from next door and bringing them to stay with the Stowaway family. And then all of the hard work began; helping the Longears build their new home in the garage at 48 Spring Blossom Road, and making it safe and comfortable for all fifteen of them. Because the Longears family had lost everything in the flood and because there were only two adults next door – Gertrude and Clem Longears. It would have taken them such a long time to sort out a new house and furniture without help from kind neighbours.

To tell the truth, the **plan** was a good one in another way too. It gave the grown-up Stowaways a project to think about and work on, now that there were no more travelling adventures. As for Valletta, well now she often had an important job to do, being 'on guard duty.'

But there were other things happening too, like **settling in** for the Tunefullys, so let's go back to a day or two after they arrived.

Valletta and Oslo were in Oslo's room with the two newcomers. Nancy was standing in the doorway, hoping that, if she was very quiet, no one would mind her being there. Vienna was in the kitchen, but she kept popping in, and then popping out again. Because she was a motherly, welcoming, kind sort of mouse and wanted to make sure Kendal and Ireleth were settling in, but because she was also a bit curious about the trunk.

'What's in it?' she wondered.

Kendal had lifted up the lid of the old trunk and now it was propped wide open against the bedroom wall. He and his sister began taking everything out.

There was a pile of smooth pebbles 'for skimming across puddles,' said Kendal.

There was a huge mountain of prickly pine cones for bonfires and campfires and well, any kind of fires. 'Very useful for camping trips,' said Kendal.

There was a music stand, (the folding sort), a mouse-sized carved wooden sword and a mouse-sized skipping rope.

'Oh, oh, oh,' said Valletta and Nancy together. 'Will you show us how to skip please?'

And there were sheets and sheets of soggy white paper where you could see there had once been music or music and words written, but now there were just a few faint squiggles left.

'They're not all spoilt,' said Ireleth. Valletta wondered how she could be so cheerful, despite everything. 'And I have a plan for the music which is ruined. It will become wallpaper.'

Valletta, Vienna, Oslo and Nancy looked a bit puzzled. Kendal didn't look at all surprised.

'Wallpaper,' said Ireleth. 'For all your bedrooms. If you'd like it, of course.'

'Well, I want some,' said Valletta.

'Me too,' said Nancy.

'And Florence,' said Ireleth, 'the grown-up artist mouse, well she can help us with making the glue and doing the sticking. She's bound to be good at that.'

So it happened that, for the next few days, the mice who weren't busy with the Longears family, were busy doing something else with Ireleth; pegging out the sheets of music which had been spoilt by the floodwater.

The wallpapering project was a huge success. Florence, even though she was busy with the Longears family, did find time to make the glue, and everyone helped with the sticking.

Or some of the sticking, because there was also learning to skip, which the three girl mice spent a lot of time doing. Nancy mostly fell over the skipping rope but she didn't mind at all. Florence also cut out pictures for the youngest four mice and gave them each a little pot of leftover glue for them to dip their tails and paws into and just have fun sticking.

And, while all this was happening, Oslo and Kendal were nowhere to be seen.

But what else was in the trunk? There were musical instruments: penny whistles, a fiddle and a colourful old accordion. There was a small rug which didn't take long to dry. Oslo and Kendal put it between their beds after it had dried. There was another much bigger rug which hadn't been in the trunk. It had bright colours and a complicated pattern. This had been so heavy and soggy that it had taken several mice to lift it. It took nearly two weeks for this one to dry.

Then there was a rucksack made of some kind of waterproofed material. Everything in it was untouched by the flood. Perfectly dry. Everything was two beakers, a flask, a box and piles and piles of folded bus timetables, and train timetables, and timetables for ferryboats and for coaches. There was also a tiny box of matches and an even tinier folding penknife. All dry and all in Kendal's rucksack.

The very last thing in the trunk was white and see through with sewn on stars and moons.

Vienna opened it up and spread it out on Valletta's bed. It covered it completely, coming down to the floor on both sides and both ends. There was still more material piled up in folds on the floor, that they were careful not to tread on in case their paws marked it.

'Those stars and moons, children,' she said, 'that's a special kind of sewing. It's called embroidery.'

'It's very pretty,' said Nancy, who loved pretty things.

Ireleth explained to them that it had once been a curtain in a human travelling caravan, where the Tunefullys had lived for a while with their parents. This had been in happier times before they came to Spring Blossom Road and before that flood.

'It won't take long to dry,' said Vienna.

'And then it could be used for dressing up, or

making dancing tutus, or hair bows for the girl mice,' said Ireleth.

'We'll see,' said Vienna. 'It seems too lovely for playing with. This could make a veil for a bride.'

'Well we don't know any brides,' said Valletta, who was losing interest a little bit, 'so it's no use to us.'

'Valletta,' said her mother. 'These things belong to Ireleth and Kendal. They're not ours.' And she gave her a look. You know the sort.

Ireleth, Valletta, Vienna and Nancy got involved in the drying out and wiping out the inside of the trunk. Then they put things back carefully, but left the trunk open to the air.

Oslo and Kendal wandered off again with small pawfuls of things. 'Be careful, dears,' said Vienna, who was still looking at the embroidered moons and stars on the white material.

Chapter 12
Valletta is a Brave Mouse

Kendal taught Oslo to skim stones across puddles. He taught him to make a fire with pine cones in the far borders of the garden. And all the children, except Sark of course, who was too little, started playing hide and seek outside their houses, and all over the area between and around the mousehouses, below the floorboards.

This wasn't normally allowed.

'Don't worry, Auntie,' said Vienna. 'It's good that they can let off a bit of steam. They've not been on adventures for such a long time.'

'Well, if you say so,' said Great Auntie Sofia, who still looked a little bit worried, 'but when the building work stops next door, this will have to stop too.'

Because of course, while the Stowaways were helping the Longears family to build another home next door, there was also repairing and mending and making and building going on above the floorboards at Number 48 Spring Blossom Road. Builders' vans and noise and big boots. Lots of activity. Because the humans' house had to be fixed too.

'When it settles down again, ' said Great Auntie Sofia, 'we'll have to tame these wild children . They'll need to be quieter when the builders go.'

It would soon be the next Moustory Night. This would be the first since Ireleth and Kendal came to stay.

The Longears family were now happy and settled once more next door. The builders' vans had left. The mouse working party returned from their mission and Bergen packed all the tools away tidily .

One morning, the children were all together – all except Sark, who was indoors with his mum. Ireleth was with the grown-ups too.

Once again, they had all followed Kendal outside the human house and were playing in the back garden. The car had gone from the garage for the big shop, so the little mice were playing tightrope on the low garden walls, climbing up the washing line and playing swings. This was all forbidden of course, and was making Oslo just a little bit jealous as he preferred it when it was just him and Kendal. With no babysitting the younger ones.

The mice were still playing 'swings' when the car pulled back in. They all scurried back inside, bumping into Florence on their way.

'Everyone's been looking for you,' said Florence. 'Where have you been?'

Valletta, Malaga and Nancy looked guilty, but Oslo just shrugged.

So what happened next? Well, first there was going to be a party in the garage for the Longears family to say thank you to the Stowaway family. But then the grown-up mice decided to move the tea party to Bergen and Vienna's home, because it seemed too unsafe to have thirty-one mice having a tea party in a garage. Especially a garage where the door didn't quite shut properly. And the grown-up mice also worried a little bit about Kendal and Ireleth, and whether they would be unhappy if they went back to Number 48, where they had so recently lost their parents in that flood.

'Really,' Annécy said to Florence, Sofia and Vienna, 'this is more to celebrate us neighbours getting to know each other. The flood was a terrible thing, but because of it, Ireleth and Kendal have come here. And we've made friends with the Longears. And that's good because this staying at home, and staying quiet – well, it was making all of us a bit lost and a bit fed up.'

Valletta and Florence were on guard. All fifteen of the Longears came to Bergen and Vienna's for an afternoon tea party with sandwiches, ginger cake, peppermint creams, chocolate cake, flapjacks, mint tea and blackberry squash. All the lovely tea time feasting favourites. It was a happy afternoon. But, at some stage, after their tummies were full to bursting, Kendal winked at Oslo and the two of them crept away. Valletta spotted them and she and Malaga scampered after them. Nomouse noticed. Kendal had a plan.

There was ice on the pond at the end of the garden. Now this was **not a good idea**. There were humans in both houses. It was still just about daylight. So there was, of course, danger.

'Someone could see us,' said Valletta, who was feeling a bit prickly about this idea already. Kendal ignored her, dragging a lid from a 'takeaway' container down the garden to the pond. The pond was really a puddle but, to mice, it was **enormous**. It was also frozen.

'Let's jump on it and slide,' said Kendal.

Malaga, Oslo and Kendal jumped on. Malaga and Oslo looked scared, but excited. At the last moment something stopped Valletta from jumping on too. She was having a little think about life before the Tunefullys arrived. Sometimes Oslo had been boring, but he had still been her brother and she missed those old days. Oslo seemed very different since Kendal had arrived. And Kendal, well she couldn't work him out at all.

The other mice shrieked. They were moving really fast, skimming across the ice and then – disaster. The ice cracked. The little lid-boat tipped into the deep water and then all three mice were thrashing and splashing. This wasn't fun at all.

'Help,' screamed Malaga. 'I'm frightened!' Oslo and Malaga were in the water. Malaga's lower lip was trembling, in fact she was shaking all over. Her whiskers were stuck to her soggy fur. She had started to cry. Kendal managed to climb out and was crawling slowly across the splintered ice. Valletta looked around the end of the garden, frantically hoping there would be something, anything, useful for helping a small mouse to rescue her brother and her cousin. At last, at the edge of the flower bed, she saw a small piece of wood with some string attached to it. She grabbed it quickly. Clutching it between her trembling paws, she moved carefully across the ice and stretched out, throwing the end of the string into the water.

'Tie it around your tummies and hold onto the end of the string. Hold on tight.' shouted Valletta. 'And you, Kendal Tunefully, you hold onto that stick, and when I say pull, you pull, and don't you dare do anything else.'

At the third throw the string reached Oslo and, when she was sure Oslo and Malaga were both tied securely, she ran back to help Kendal pull the other two mice to land. All four shivering mice were sitting at the side of the pond, when Florence came running down the path.

'I'm not even going to ask,' she said, 'until you're all inside and you're all safe. But I am ashamed of your reckless, foolish behaviour. You could have been killed.'

Florence's beautiful eyes glittered with anger. There would be a telling off later. How could Kendal and Oslo have been so stupid? But for now, she found blankets and shawls and wrapped them all up. They were freezing, even Valletta, who hadn't been in the water. Florence led them all in a dripping procession back up to her home upstairs. The party was over. Leningrad and Sofia were there to greet them all.

Chapter 13
Snow

Three exciting things were happening, all close together. There was the tea-party, then Moustory Night, and then it would be Christmouse Day.

The humans at Number 46 always had a gigantic real Christmouse tree. It came back to the house strapped onto the roof of the red Volvo car. Then the humans carried the tree into the garage where it was trimmed and fitted into its tree-stand. This was how the Stowaways got their trees; they could make four trees for their houses out of the humans' tree trimmings.

The humans at Number 48 had an artificial tree which they brought out of the loft every December. So they had no trimmings for the mice they shared their space with. So this year the trimmings would become five trees – one for the Longears family as well.

It was Bergen, Guernsey and Jersey who collected the tree trimmings. Valletta was on guard duty with Florence. This was one of the most exciting days in the mouse year.

And while some of the mice were dragging the little branches which would become their trees, other mice were making paper chains, and more pompoms for decorating their houses.

So the trees were collected, put up and decorated and the next night was Moustory Night at Arran, Guernsey and Nancy's house. Everyone was there, all sixteen of them, and everyone brought food and drink again.

'Moustory Night at our house, hooray,' said Nancy, and then Valletta joined in with her, 'when we all spend an evening together, every full moon, and we sing our Stowaway song and all the grown-ups tell our family stories.'

'Tall tales and long tales and short tales and furry tales. True tales and very-nearly-true tales about our ancestors, about things that happened ages and ages ago, and things that happened just a little while ago,' said Great Uncle

Leningrad

'And tonight, my dears, I'll tell you about a little while ago, and about everything that's happened with our family and with the Longears family, our neighbours and friends next door. Because we have no tales of travel for you this time.'

The Stowaways who weren't in Bergen's working party hadn't seen how bad things were next door after the flood. Neither had they seen what a wonderful home Bergen's team had made for the Longears. Great Uncle Leningrad did not remind any of the mice about what had happened to Mr and Mrs Tunefully. He didn't say anything about what had happened on the ice, although all of the mice knew about it. And they knew how brave Valletta had been too. The telling off happened on the day of the accident. Great Uncle Leningrad had been very angry, but calm and sad too. He'd looked over his glasses at the four wet mice and shaken his head.

'I'm so very disappointed in you,' he said. 'especially with you two, Kendal and Oslo. I expected better, more thoughtful behaviour from you.' All of the mice squeaked, squealed and cried, except for Kendal who looked at the floor without making a sound, and flicked his tail from side to side. Nomouse knew what Kendal was thinking. Nomouse ever knew.

'That boy must know what he did and how dangerous it was. We don't need to remind him and make him feel uncomfortable at a Moustory Night,' Leningrad had said to Sofia earlier that evening. Sofia frowned. She didn't agree but she kept this to herself.

Ireleth sang Christmouse carols and songs and played her accordion. They all joined in with Away in a Manger, We Will Rock You, Little Donkey and We Wish You a Merry Christmouse. Kendal played the fiddle. Nancy jumped up and down excitedly and twirled in circles until she felt dizzy. Oslo, Jersey and Guernsey played the penny whistle.

And then everyone said the Stowaway rhyme together, even Ireleth. Valletta was watching Kendal. He was quiet and didn't join in.

'We're the Stowaways, the Stowaways;
we like to travel, to go away.
We creep into their bags and cases

and then we visit lovely places.
We can go by car, or go by bus;
all kinds of boats are fine with us,
and if our humans ride by train,
we little mice do not complain.
Just beware if they talk of flights!
Those metal birds give mice a fright!'

The three youngest children were very sleepy. Annécy and Jersey scooped up their two and said their goodnights, very softly. Arran left the room carrying Nancy, who had fallen asleep on Ireleth's lap. She didn't even squeak when he tucked the blanket round her whiskers.

The next day was Christmouse Day. The Stowaways had already had two parties, but there was still more feasting. They sang songs and recited poems about mice, reindeers and Father Christmouse. Then they played charades and did a jigsaw puzzle Bergen and Guernsey had made, (showing a table full of food and drink,) for everyone to work on together.

In the evening, Florence brought out the Stowaway

map for all the grown-ups to look at.

'Maybe next year, my dears…' said Leningrad. 'Maybe the adventures will start again next year.'

It was a good but a quiet Christmouse. Ireleth's eyes were sad but you could only tell if you stood really close to her. Guernsey noticed.

Arran wished everyone **a very happy Christmouse**, and went to bed a little earlier than the other adult mice. He always felt a bit unhappy at this time of year, since the loss of Nancy's mum, his lovely Shannon.

And then two mornings after Christmouse, very, very early, Valletta was sitting all by herself in the air brick . It was cold and she was wrapped in a blanket. Her breath made wispy patterns in the air and it felt like her whiskers were starting to freeze.

There had been snow in the night. It started just as the youngest mice had been put to bed. Valletta watched thick flakes of snow fall for a while. It had been nearly a year of staying at home and not doing the things they used to do, but this was wonderful: a big, soft, white blanket of loveliness.

Later they would all find a safe way for the little ones to have some fun in the snow. But safe fun, with someone being on guard. Not like that awful afternoon on the ice with Kendal. Valletta shuddered as she remembered that day.

There were two voices behind her. It was her father, Bergen and her brother, Oslo. They all sat wrapped in blankets in the airbrick and watched the snow together. It was that still time of the morning before everyone else woke up, and the world outside looked so beautiful.

And then Valletta saw them. Footprints. Small footprints in the snow. There were mouse footprints in the snow leading away down to the gate and out into Spring Blossom Road. A small paw reached for her paw. It was Oslo and his eyes were glittering, as if he was trying not to cry.

'It's Kendal,' Oslo said quietly. 'He went in the night and he took the rucksack. You know, with all his maps and timetables, and that little rug off the floor. And his fiddle. He knew I was awake but he didn't say anything. He didn't even say goodbye.'

'I think he was probably feeling guilty about the ice accident,' said Bergen gently. 'He did put you all in danger and he should have known better.' Oslo and Valletta looked a bit sad and confused.

'But you know something,' said Bergen, 'I don't think he would have stayed anyway. He's not the staying, settling kind of mouse.'

'He was my friend,' said Oslo, very quietly this time.

'I know he was,' Valletta whispered, and squeezed his paw for a moment. 'What about Ireleth?' she asked. 'Do you think she'll leave us too?'

'I don't think so,' said Bergen. 'I think she's happy with us. And like your mother says – 'watch this space.'

Then he gave both his children a hug. 'I'm going to make your mum up a nice cup of tea, and then later we can play snowballs and make a snowmouse. When it's safe.'

Valletta and Oslo sat side by side wrapped up in blankets and looked at the snow falling. There had been some good things this year. They did have each other. And they were not ordinary mice.

They were the Stowaways.

Simone Mansell Broome

Simone Mansell Broome was born in, and now lives back in, West Wales. There was a long time in the middle of living in other places.

She is a published poet with two full-length collections, one slim volume and an ebook, and has also published an ebook based on her lockdown blog.

Valletta and the Year of Changes is her first adventure into the world of children's fiction.

simone@simonemansellbroome.com